What does Emma the babysitter make?

What does Ian play with?

What does Ian make for Sarah?

What does Ian eat to get better?

Which bed is Ian's bed?

What does Ian drink from? And Mom?

Which clothes does Ian wear to bed?

First published in Belgium and Holland by Clavis Uitgeverij, Hasselt – Amsterdam, 2015
Copyright © 2015, Clavis Uitgeverij

English translation from the Dutch by Clavis Publishing Inc. New York
Copyright © 2017 for the English language edition: Clavis Publishing Inc. New York

Visit us on the web at www.clavisbooks.com

Ian Is Sick written and illustrated by Pauline Oud
Original title: *Kas is ziek*
Translated from the Dutch by Clavis Publishing

ISBN 978-1-60537-325-6

This book was printed in April 2017 at Publikum d.o.o., Slavka Rodica 6, Belgrade, Serbia

First Edition
10 9 8 7 6 5 4 3 2 1

Ian Is Sick

Pauline Oud

Clavis

NEW YORK

Ian can't stop coughing.
His throat hurts. He doesn't want to eat.
And Ian doesn't feel like playing either.
Mom feels his forehead. Ian is burning up.
He has a fever.

"Come on, Ian," says Mom.
"You're sick and you're going to bed.
Take off your clothes and put on your pajamas."
Mom tucks Ian in and gives him a big kiss.
Ian coughs a few times and then he falls asleep.

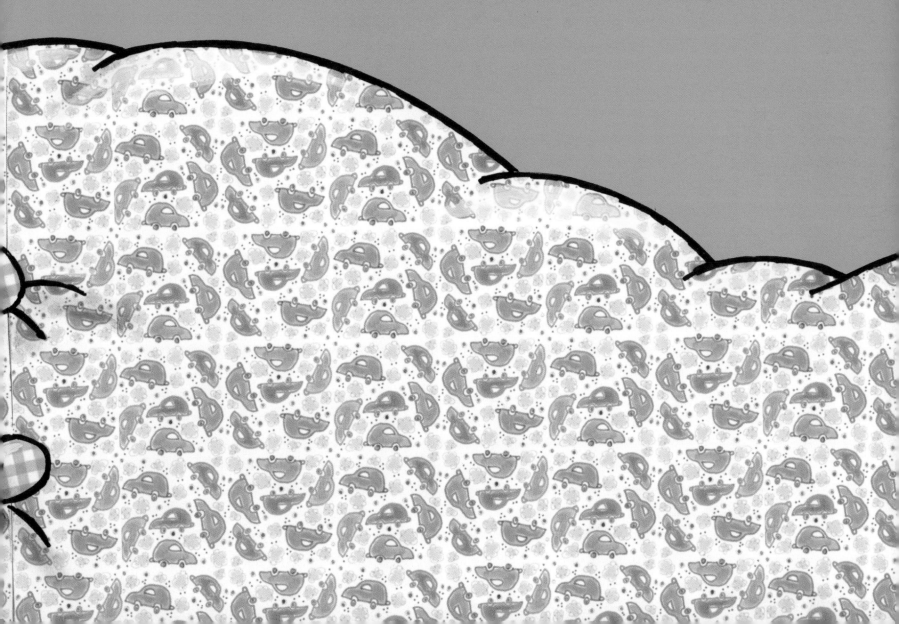

Dad goes to the doctor for cough medicine and pills.
The cough medicine is sweet, but the pill doesn't taste good.
Luckily the pill helps. Ian soon feels a bit better.
Mom makes a cozy little bed on the couch for Ian,
with his blanket that has little cars on it.
Ian can sit on Mom's lap for a while. That's nice.

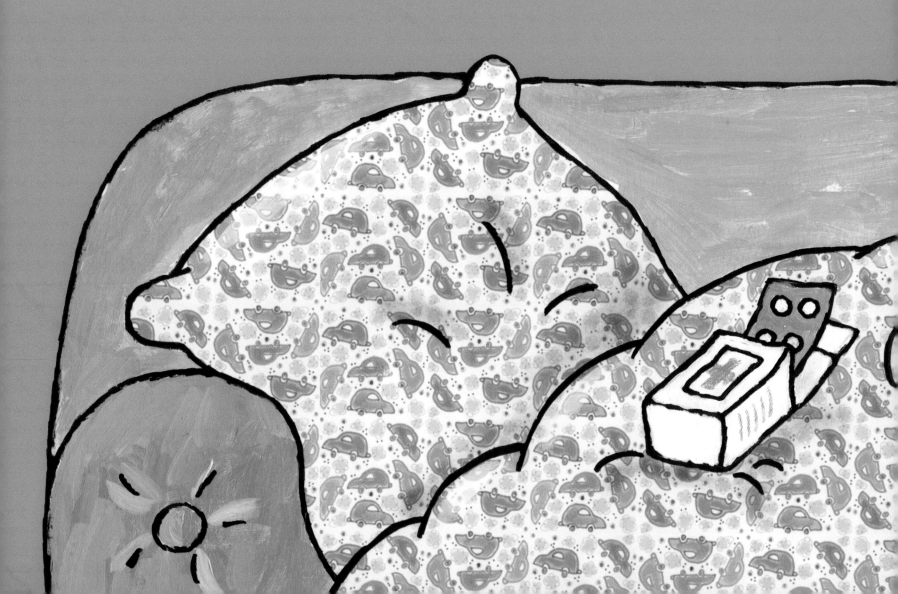

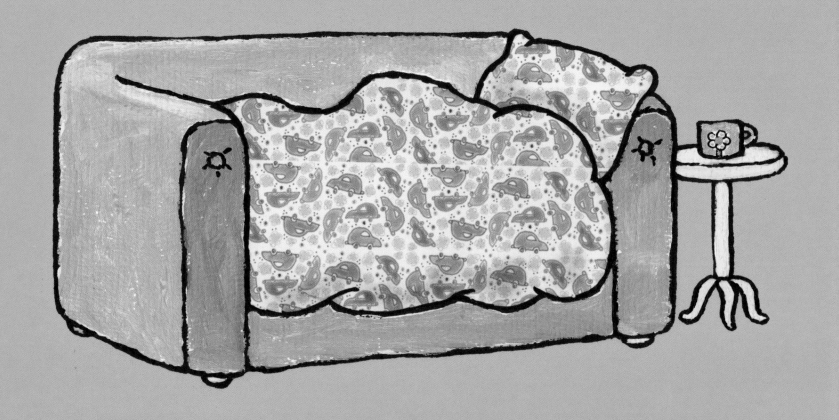

Ian can't go to school today.

And Mom and Dad have to go to work.

"Ding dong!" goes the doorbell. Mom opens the door.

"My name is Emma. I'm the babysitter," says a woman
with long hair to Ian. "You must be Ian."

"I'm sick," says Ian shyly.

"Good!" says babysitter Emma. "Then I can use
magic to make you better."

"Can you really do magic?" Ian asks.
"I sure can," laughs Emma. "Wait and see!"
But first they wave good-bye to Mom.
"Bye, Mom!" Ian barely looks at her;
he is busy playing cards with Emma.

Ian shows Emma all his books.
She reads for as long as Ian wants.
After Ian has slept for a while, Emma takes some eggs
and milk from the fridge.
"Now watch closely, Ian. I'm going to do some magic!
Hocus-pocus... I wish Ian were better!" Emma makes
her special pancakes.
Mmmmm! Ian eats the pancakes and soon feels better!

"You look a lot better, Ian!"
Mom says cheerfully when she comes home.
Ian laughs and tells her all about Emma's
magic pancakes.
Then Mom and Ian say good-bye to Emma.
"Bye, Emma! Thanks for the great day
and for your magic!"
"Bye, Ian!"

The magic pancakes worked!
Ian's throat is feeling better.
But he is a little bored.
Luckily Sarah, the girl
next door, comes to visit!
Ian and Sarah make
a high tower together.

The next day Ian is feeling all better.
He doesn't have to cough anymore.
He is eating and having fun playing again.
"Can I go and play at Sarah's, Mom?" Ian asks.
"Of course! Go get your coat and shoes!" says Mom.
Mom and Ian walk to Sarah's house together.

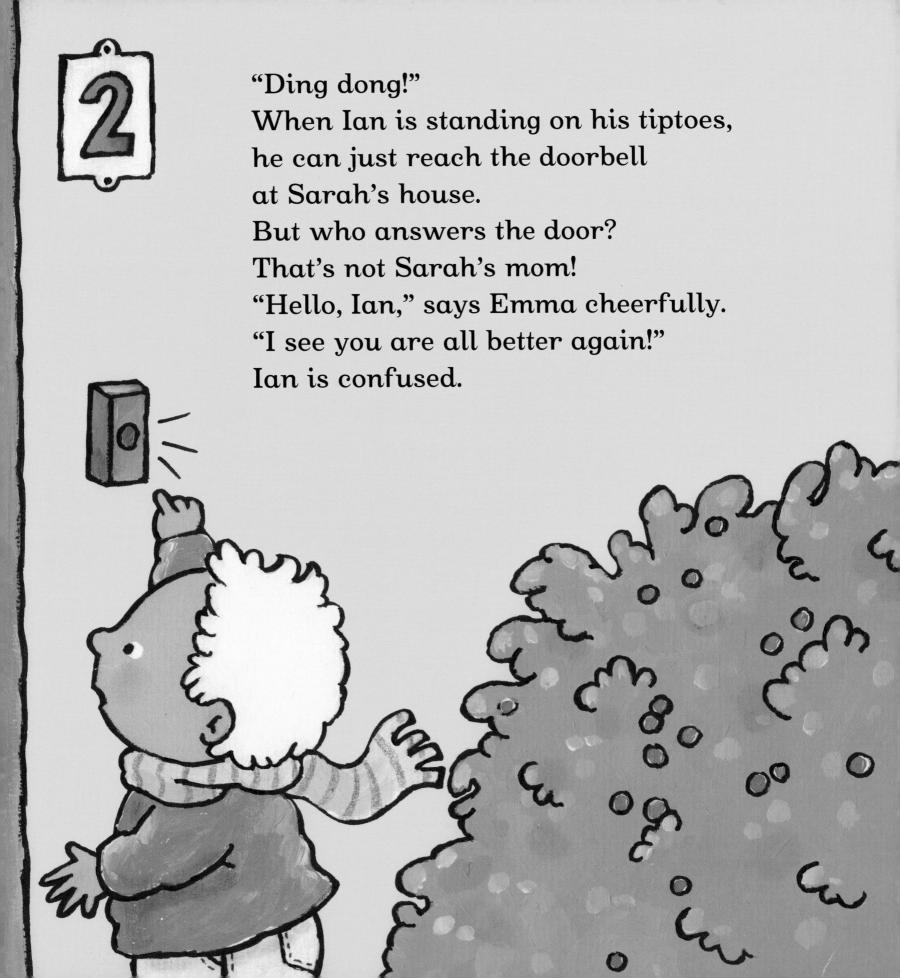

"Ding dong!"
When Ian is standing on his tiptoes,
he can just reach the doorbell
at Sarah's house.
But who answers the door?
That's not Sarah's mom!
"Hello, Ian," says Emma cheerfully.
"I see you are all better again!"
Ian is confused.

"Come on in," says Emma.
What does Ian hear?
"Cough... cough!" Who is coughing like that?
Sarah is lying on the couch.

She coughs, she doesn't want to eat and she has a fever....
"Now Sarah is sick," says Emma.
Ian can stay with Sarah for a little while.
"I was sick too, Sarah.
But now I'm all better!"

"Look, Sarah," says Ian. "I made you something."
Ian drew a very pretty card with a big heart on it.
For Sarah, who's sick!

And what do Ian and Sarah smell?
"Emma made magic pancakes!" Ian says happily.
"You'll feel better in
no time, Sarah!"